To Ann & Kelly

Merry Christmas

Fondly,

Joyce

W9-AXS-371

CARL'S CHRISTMAS

A SCHOLASTIC BOOK CLUB EDITION

Carl's Christmas

ALEXANDRA DAY

FARRAR STRAUS GIROUX · NEW YORK

To Toby,
the real Carl

Copyright © 1990 by Alexandra Day
All rights reserved
Library of Congress catalog card number 90-55164
Published in Canada by HarperCollins*CanadaLtd*
Color separations by Imago Sales USA, Inc.
Printed and bound in Hong Kong by Imago Sales USA, Inc.
First edition, 1990
Third printing, 1991

The Carl character originally appeared in *Good Dog, Carl* by
Alexandra Day, published by Green Tiger Press

0-590-44790-4

"We're going to Grandma's and then to church.
Take good care of the baby, Carl."

Be our 1,000th customer and win this beautiful CHRISTMAS BASKET